Grandpa's
Magic Slippers

Christopher Palmer

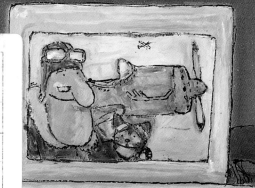

For my mother, father and brother, Tim
C. P.

First published in 2004 in Great Britain by Gullane Children's Books
This paperback edition published in 2005 by
Gullane Children's Books
an imprint of Pinwheel Limited
Winchester House, 259-269 Old Marylebone Road,
London NW1 5XJ

1 3 5 7 9 10 8 6 4 2

Text and illustrations © Christopher Palmer 2004

The right of Christopher Palmer to be identified
as the author and illustrator of this work has been asserted by him
in accordance with the Copyright, Designs and Patents Act, 1988.

A CIP record for this title is available from the British Library.

ISBN 1 86233 346 7 hardback
ISBN 1 86233 536 2 paperback

Grandpa's Magic Slippers

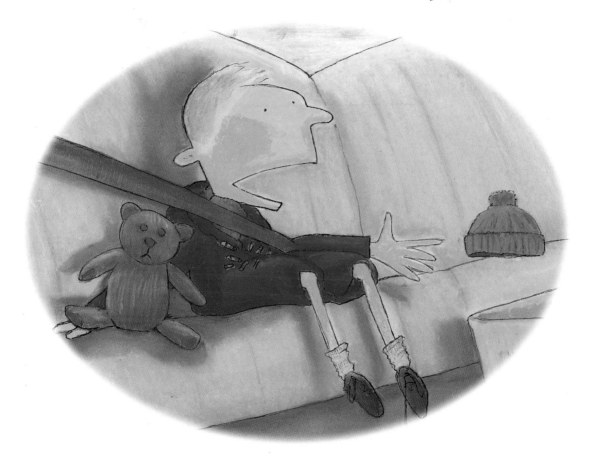

Christopher Palmer

GULLANE
CHILDREN'S BOOKS

"But Mum, I don't want to go to Grandpa's," moaned Charlie. "He's always asleep and he smells funny."

"I'm sorry, Charlie," his mother replied, "but I have to visit your Aunt Susan at the hospital, and I'm running late so, come on, let's get you inside quickly . . ."

"Now, Grandpa's just having a little nap, so why don't you play with your toys quietly and I'll be back in an hour." And with that, his mother was gone.

Charlie was bored. It was no fun when Grandpa was asleep and he couldn't even find Alfie to play with.

"Oh! Hello,
Charlie my boy . . ."

"Hello, Grandpa. I hope I didn't wake you. I've been looking everywhere for Alfie but I can't find him!"

"Oh! That troublesome cat! I must have left him behind on my last trip," said Grandpa.

Charlie looked puzzled. He didn't think Grandpa ever went anywhere.

"Come on, there's only one thing for it, Charlie . . . I could use your help!"

Grandpa's slippers gave out a blinding **FLASH !**

. . . the room began to spin round and round . . . .

Charlie blinked and rubbed his eyes.
Grandpa's sitting room had disappeared –
they were in the middle of the desert!

"Wow! How did we get here, Grandpa?"
asked Charlie.
Grandpa grinned. "With my magic slippers,
of course! Come on, we must find Alfie."

They rode across the desert towards an oasis.
"Look at that huge tent, Grandpa! Maybe
Alfie's hiding in there?"
"Good thinking, Charlie – let's go
and have a look."

"There he is, Grandpa!"
cried Charlie excitedly,
"I can see his tail."

The slippers gave out
another **FLASH!** and
before Charlie could say anything,
the tent began to spin round and
round . . .

"That was close! Where are we now, Grandpa?"
"Why, I think we're in the Arctic, Charlie!"
"Look, Grandpa – footprints!
Alfie must be in the igloo!"

But as they crawled inside . . . "Whoa!" shouted Charlie, "a bear!
Quick, Grandpa, use your magic slippers!"

"Weeheeee! This is fun!" cried Charlie.
"I think I can hear Alfie purring! Listen, Grandpa!"

But it wasn't Alfie who was purring . . .

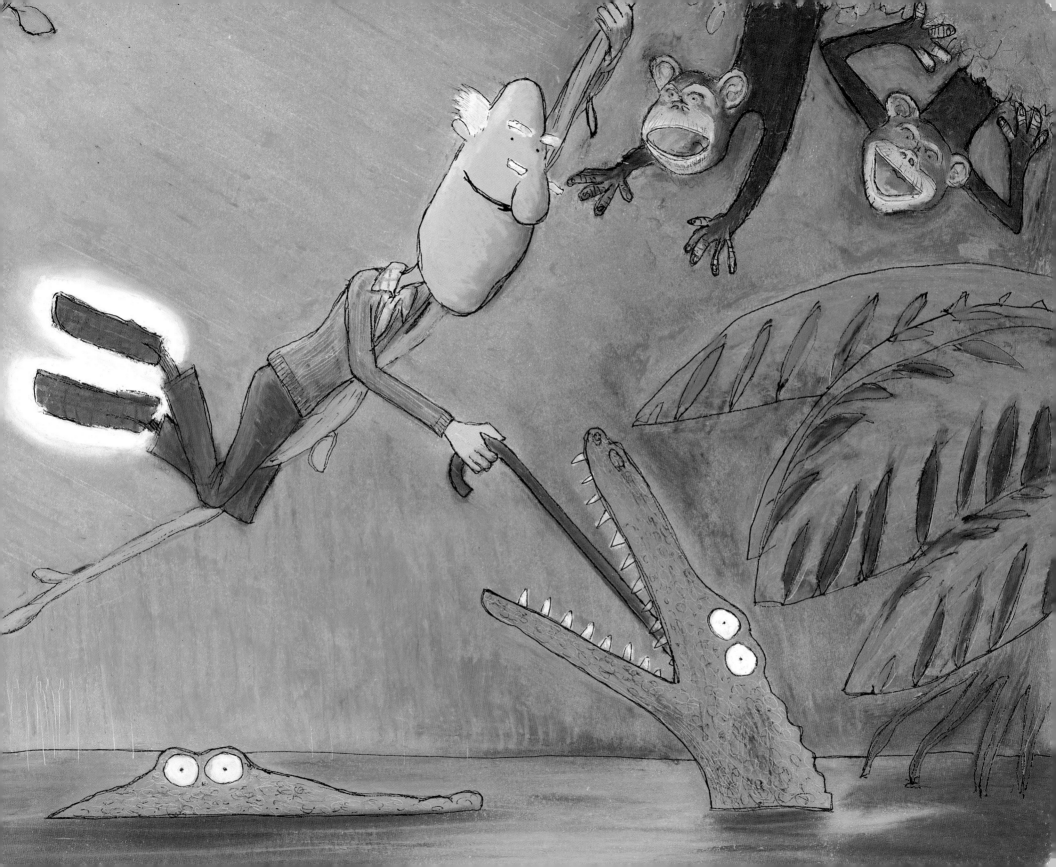

"G-g-g-grandpa! We need your slippers again . . ."
stuttered Charlie.
"Don't worry, I'll just wriggle
my toes, and . . .

. . . Phew! Just in the nick of time, my boy!
Now where are we?"
  "I don't like this cave, Grandpa."
  "No, neither do I! I think it's time
to go home, Charlie!"

In an instant, they were back in Grandpa's sitting room – weary and tired, but safe and sound.

"It's nice to be home, but we still haven't found Alfie. And look, Grandpa! You've lost one of your slippers!" said Charlie.

"Goodness me! I must have dropped it in the cave. We haven't got time to go back. Your mother will be here in a minute . . ."

And with that the doorbell rang.

"Hello, you two. Look who I found on the doorstep."
It was Alfie!
"What on earth is he doing with your
old slipper?" asked Charlie's mother.

"Alfie! You clever thing!" chuckled Grandpa.
And, as Alfie padded over to the fire,
he caught Charlie's eye and gave
him just the tiniest wink . . .